Heartstrings and Rhymes

A Collection of Poetry

Sayan Panda

Ukiyoto Publishing

All global publishing rights are held by

Ukiyoto Publishing

Published in 2024

Content Copyright © Sayan Panda

ISBN 9789361728761

*All rights reserved.
No part of this publication may be reproduced,
transmitted, or stored in a retrieval system, in any form
by any means, electronic, mechanical, photocopying,
recording or otherwise, without the prior permission of
the publisher.*

The moral rights of the authors have been asserted.

*This is a work of fiction. Names, characters, businesses,
places, events, locales, and incidents are either the
products of the author's imagination or used in a fictitious
manner. Any resemblance to actual persons, living or
dead, or actual events is purely coincidental.*

*This book is sold subject to the condition that it shall not by
way of trade or otherwise, be lent, resold, hired out or
otherwise circulated, without the publisher's prior
consent, in any form of binding or cover other than that in
which it is published.*

www.ukiyoto.com

To the one who taught me how to love truly.

Contents

Binding Hearts	1
Seasonal Love	2
Shared Glances	3
Sculpture of our Love	5
Tapestry of Love	7
Rhythm Changes	9
The Labyrinth of Love	11
Eternal Connection	13
Slumber's Realm	14
Alchemy of Love	15
Architect of Love	17
Navigating Love	19
Threads of Love	21
Kaleidoscope	22
Forgotten Moments	24
Symphony of Love	26
Love Library	28
Elemental Love	30
Celestial Love	32
Love in a Time Capsule	33
Physics of Love	35
About the Author	*37*

Binding Hearts

In the depths of my soul, love gently stirred,
A flickering ember, waiting to be heard.

Passion ignited, a flame began to grow,
Love's warmth enveloping, a gentle glow.

Amidst the chaos, love found its way,
A beacon of hope, guiding night into day.

Through the stormy seas, love held me tight,
A steadfast anchor, in the darkest of night.

Whispers of affection, soft as a breeze,
Love's gentle touch, putting my heart at ease.

In your embrace, all worries subside,
Love's tender embrace, a place to confide.

Each passing moment, love's bond grew strong,
A symphony of emotions, an eternal song.

In the tapestry of time, love weaves its thread,
Binding hearts together, where eternity is spread.

Seasonal Love

In the spring's embrace, our love takes flight,
Like blossoms blooming, radiant and bright.
With each new day, our hearts awaken,
As nature's beauty, our love is taken.

In the summer's heat, our love burns strong,
Like the sun's rays, passionate and long.
Under the azure skies, we find our bliss,
In the warmth of love's eternal kiss.

In the autumn's breeze, our love transforms,
Like leaves that change, in colors it conforms.
Through seasons of change, our love remains,
An evergreen bond, that nothing can restrain.

In the winter's hush, our love finds solace,
Like snowflakes falling, in peaceful embrace.
In quiet moments, our hearts intertwine,
Love's whispers echoing, in a world so fine.

Through the changing seasons, our love evolves,
Each chapter written, as our story revolves.
In spring, summer, autumn, and winter's embrace,
Our love endures, filled with boundless grace.

Shared Glances

In the quiet spaces between our words,
Where the whispers of love are heard,
Lie the moments that truly define,
The rhythm of our love, so divine.

In synchronized heartbeats, we find,
A symphony composed by souls entwined,
With every thump, a love song plays,
Echoing the depth of our affection's blaze.

Shared glances, like secret codes,
Speak volumes without words, they impose,
A language known only to our hearts,
A dance of emotions, where love imparts.

In the stillness of a tender touch,
We feel the power of love's gentle clutch,
Fingers interlaced, a sacred connection,
Binding our souls in a loving reflection.

In the silence of a stolen kiss,
We taste the sweetness of eternal bliss,
Lips pressed together, a moment suspended,
A universe created, where love is splendid.

These intimate moments, often unseen,
Are the threads that weave our love's serene,
They create the rhythm of our dance,
An unspoken language, a true romance.

So let us cherish these moments so dear,
For in them, the beauty of love appears,
In synchronized heartbeats and shared glances,
We find the magic that love enhances.

As our love's rhythm continues to play,
May it grow stronger with each passing day,
For in these small, quiet moments we share,
Lies the depth of a love beyond compare.

Sculpture of our Love

In the canvas of our love, colors intertwine,
A masterpiece painted, divine and fine,
Each stroke of passion, a vibrant hue,
A reflection of our love, ever anew.

Like a dance, our love takes graceful form,
Swirling and twirling, through calm and storm,
In steps of tenderness, we find our way,
A choreography of love, night and day.

As a symphony, our love orchestrates,
Melodies of emotions, love resonates,
From soft whispers to crescendos high,
Our hearts harmonize, never shy.

In the sculpture of our love, we mold,
Carving out a love story, yet untold,
Hands shaping the contours of our hearts,
A masterpiece evolving, where love imparts.

Just like a piece of music, our love evolves,
With moments of inspiration, it resolves,
The sweet melodies that fill the air,
Creating a love song, beyond compare.

But like any art, our love faces trials,
Moments of frustration that test our smiles,
Yet through it all, we triumph and rise,
A testament to love's enduring ties.

Our love, a masterpiece, forever in progress,
An ever-evolving work of art, no less,
With each passing day, we add a touch,
Creating a love that's cherished so much.

So let us embrace this artistry of love,
With every stroke, note, step, and curve,
For in the complexity, beauty is found,
Our love, a masterpiece, forever renowned.

Tapestry of Love

In the depths of darkness, love becomes a light,
Guiding us through the toughest of nights,
With silent strength, it holds us tight,
A beacon of hope, shining so bright.

Through trials and tribulations, hand in hand we stand,
Supporting each other, a steadfast band,
In the face of adversity, we rise above,
Bound by a love that's unbreakable, like a glove.

Silent sacrifices made, without a word,
A testament to the love that's undisturbed,
In selflessness, we find our greatest might,
For love is the fuel that ignites our fight.

Through storms and tempests, we remain strong,
Together, we endure, and carry on,
With hearts intertwined, we find solace and peace,
A sanctuary of love that will never cease.

In the unspoken understanding, our souls connect,
A language beyond words, no need to dissect,
We feel each other's pain, we share each other's joy,

A bond so deep, no force can destroy.

In the face of adversity, love becomes our shield,
A fortress of strength, a power revealed,
With resilience as our armor, we face the unknown,
United in love, we'll never be alone.

So let us honor the quiet strength we possess,
In the battles we fight, in the trials we address,
For love is the anchor that keeps us secure,
A force that endures, forever pure.

In the tapestry of our love, strength is woven,
Through every thread, our bond unbroken,
With every challenge, our love grows stronger,
A testament to the enduring power we harbor.

So let us celebrate the strength love bestows,
In the quiet moments, where resilience shows,
For in the depths of love, we find our might,
A force that withstands, radiating light.

Rhythm Changes

Love, a dance of souls entwined,
With rhythmic steps and movements kind.
A waltz of hearts in perfect tune,
From graceful glides to spins in swoon.

Embracing closeness, bodies sway,
In syncopated rhythm they play.
A tango's passion fills the air,
As fiery gazes meet and dare.

A ballet of grace and elegance,
Love's pirouettes in grand entrance.
Each movement tells a tale untold,
Of love's desires, bold and bold.

But love's dance can sometimes falter,
Awkward steps, a stumble or alter.
Yet partners learn to find their way,
In harmony they gently sway.

The rhythm changes, the tempo shifts,
Love's dance a journey that uplifts.
Through dips and turns, they find their groove,
A rhythm only they can prove.

And as the music softly fades,
Love's dance endures, forever cascades.
A symphony of love, a beautiful sight,
Two souls entwined, dancing through the night.

So let love be a dance, forever anew,
With rhythms, steps, and movements true.
May the dance of love, forever endure,
A timeless bond, forever pure.

The Labyrinth of Love

In the labyrinth of love, we embark,
A journey of twists and turns, in the dark.
A complex maze that tests our will,
Challenges and discoveries, we fulfill.

At the entrance, excitement fills the air,
With hope and anticipation, we dare.
The path ahead, uncertain and unknown,
But together, we navigate, hand in hand we're shown.

The first turn, a rush of emotions collide,
As we encounter love's passionate stride.
The flames of desire, burning bright and strong,
Igniting our hearts, carrying us along.

But soon we reach a fork in the road,
Choices to make, a decision bestowed.
Do we take the path of trust and devotion?
Or venture down the path of doubt and commotion?

We choose the former, with hearts aligned,
Building a foundation, steadfast and kind.
Through obstacles and hurdles, we persist,
Love's labyrinth, a journey we insist.

As we wander deeper into the maze,
We face the shadows of doubt and haze.
But with each challenge, we grow stronger,
Learning to communicate, to forgive, and to ponder.

Sometimes we stumble, losing our way,
But love's compass guides us, day by day.
We find solace in the laughter we share,
And the moments of vulnerability we bear.

The labyrinth of love, it tests our resolve,
Teaching us lessons, evolving as we evolve.
Through its intricate twists and turns,
Our love forges, deepens, and yearns.

And as we reach the center, hand in hand,
We realize that love's labyrinth was planned.
Every twist and turn, every unexpected path,
Led us closer together, in love's aftermath.

So let us embrace the journey we've taken,
Through the labyrinth of love, never forsaken.
For it is in the challenges we've overcome,
That our love's labyrinth shall forever be sung.

Eternal Connection

In the flowing river of our love, I find solace,
A gentle current that carries us, hand in hand.
Like the ebb and flow of the water's embrace,
Our love remains constant, steadfast, and grand.

As sturdy as a mountain, our love stands tall,
With roots that run deep, anchoring our souls.
Through storms and trials, we will never fall,
Together we conquer, our love forever unfolds.

Like a tree, our love continues to grow,
Branches reaching high, embracing the sky.
With each passing season, our affection will show,
Blossoming with beauty, never questioning why.

For in nature's realm, we find our reflection,
The river, the mountain, the tree, all intertwined.
Symbolizing the depths of our affection,
A love eternal, forever entwined.

Now, let the winds carry this poem to your heart,
May it resonate with the beauty of our love's art.
For in the parallels of nature and affection,
We find the essence of our eternal connection.

Slumber's Realm

In dreams, love takes flight on wings unseen,
Whispering secrets in the moonlit night.
Desires dance, entwined in a cosmic beam,
As hearts embrace, guided by starlight.

In slumber's realm, fears find their release,
Conjuring shadows that seek to divide.
But love, undeterred, brings a sense of peace,
Conquering darkness with a love that's tried.

Fantasies unfurl like blossoms in bloom,
Painting landscapes of passion untamed.
Two souls entwined, defying all gloom,
In dreamscapes where eternal love is named.

In dreams, love's essence transcends the real,
Boundless and infinite, it knows no end.
A symphony of emotions that we feel,
Where dreams and love in harmony blend.

So let us wander in the realm of dreams,
Where love's enchantment forever streams.
In surreal visions, love's beauty gleams,
As desires and fantasies find their themes.

Alchemy of Love

Love, the alchemy of hearts,
Transforms the ordinary into art,
An elixir that weaves its spell,
Turning moments into stories to tell.

Like the alchemist's touch, love's embrace,
Transmutes the base to golden grace,
In the crucible of passion's fire,
Two souls entwined, reaching higher.

From leaden hearts, love extracts,
The hidden gold, the purest acts,
The dross of doubt and fear it melts,
Revealing treasures that love compels.

Love's alchemy, a wondrous thing,
A potion that makes our spirits sing,
It turns the mundane into the sublime,
Creating a world where all is prime.

Just as the alchemist seeks to find,
The philosopher's stone, the elixir kind,
Love seeks to transform and refine,
Making hearts glow, like gold that shines.

So let us cherish this alchemical power,
That transforms us in each passing hour,
For love, like alchemy's magical art,
Can turn the ordinary into a work of heart.

As the alchemist seeks to transmute,
Base metals into gold, absolute,
Love transmutes the ordinary, it's true,
Into something extraordinary, just for you.

Architect of Love

In the realm of love, we lay the foundation strong,
Building a life together, where we both belong.
Like architects of hearts, we design with care,
Constructing a bond that's meant to forever bear.

The walls we raise are built on trust and respect,
With bricks of understanding, we never neglect.
We lay each stone with tenderness and grace,
Crafting a structure that time cannot erase.

Through the seasons of life, we weather the storm,
Renovating our love, keeping it safe and warm.
With every challenge faced, we strengthen our ties,
Creating a love that only grows and never dies.

Our love is the blueprint, a masterpiece so grand,
A collaborative construction, hand in hand.
With every beam and pillar, our love stands tall,
Together we build, united, we'll never fall.

As years go by, our love continues to grow,
A testament to the foundation we laid long ago.
We build a life of joy, laughter, and bliss,
Creating a love story that's truly timeless.

So let us keep building, constructing with care,
For love is the architecture we both share.
With every brick and beam, we'll build our dreams,
Creating a love that forever gleams.

Navigating Love

Ah, the vast and ever-changing seascape of love,
Where calm surfaces hide stormy depths below.
A metaphor so fitting, like a hand in glove,
For the emotions that ebb and flow.

Love, like the sea, has its tranquil moments,
Where the surface glistens with peaceful grace.
But beneath, there lie uncharted components,
A realm of passion and desire, a secret place.

In the depths of love, emotions run deep,
Like powerful currents that surge and sway.
Turbulent waves, like emotions that seep,
Can overwhelm and sweep us away.

Yet, amidst the tempest, love still sails,
Navigating through the tumultuous sea.
With steadfast hearts, it never fails,
To find its course, to set hearts free.

Love's adventurous spirit takes us far and wide,
Exploring uncharted territories, unknown.
With each new horizon, we cannot hide,
From the exhilaration that love has sown.

So let us embrace the sea of love,
With all its beauty, mystery, and strife.
For it is in this vast expanse above,
That we truly experience the meaning of life.

In love's vast seascape, we find our way,
Through tranquil waters and storms that roar.
For it is in love's depths, come what may,
That we discover the treasures worth fighting for.

Threads of Love

The threads of love, unseen, yet strong and true,
Bind us together, me and you.
Through shared experiences, our tapestry grows,
Creating a bond that only our hearts know.

Each thread represents a moment in time,
A memory cherished, forever intertwined.
The laughter we shared, the tears we shed,
The trust that blossomed as our love spread.

These threads are woven with understanding and care,
A testament to the love we both bear.
They hold us close, even when we're apart,
Binding our souls, never to depart.

In the depths of our hearts, the threads intertwine,
Forming a fabric that is solely yours and mine.
Through life's trials and storms that may come,
Our love remains steadfast, never undone.

So let these invisible threads be our guide,
As we journey together, side by side.
For in this tapestry of love, we find,
A connection unbreakable, one of a kind.

Kaleidoscope

In the canvas of love, let colors unfold,
A spectrum of emotions, a tale to be told.
From fiery reds of passion, burning so bright,
To calming blues of trust, a gentle delight.

The first stroke of love, a blush of rosy pink,
A tender affection, the beginning, we think.
With hearts all aflutter, like petals in bloom,
Exploring new feelings, dispelling all gloom.

As time goes on, the colors start to change,
From passionate reds, to a deeper orange.
The flame of desire, burning steady and strong,
Igniting the souls as they journey along.

But love is not always a fiery affair,
Sometimes it's a yellow, a warmth in the air.
A gentle glow of happiness, like the sun's golden rays,
Filling hearts with joy, brightening their days.

And then comes the green, symbol of growth,
Nurturing the love, helping it both to grow.
Through challenges and trials, it stands the test,
A resilient bond, in which both can rest.

But love isn't always smooth, it can be gray,
Clouded by doubts, causing hearts to sway.
Yet even in darkness, a silver lining appears,
A glimmer of hope, that can conquer all fears.

And in the depths of love, there's a shade of blue,
A tranquil serenity, a sense of being true.
A calm and peacefulness, that comes from within,
A love that's secure, where hearts can begin.

And as the journey continues, colors intertwine,
Creating a masterpiece, a love so divine.
From passionate reds to calming blues,
Every shade tells a story, every hue.

So let love be a canvas, painted with care,
With colors of emotions, a vibrant affair.
May your love story be a masterpiece of art,
A kaleidoscope of colors, a reflection of your heart.

Forgotten Moments

Ah, the beauty of the small, forgotten moments,
Hidden gems overshadowed by grand events.
In the tapestry of love, they find their place,
Brief exchanges, subtle glances, acts of grace.

A stolen gaze across the crowded room,
Eyes meeting, speaking without a word.
A gentle touch, a brush of fingertips,
Whispering love that only the heart heard.

A shared smile over a private joke,
Laughter bubbling up from deep within.
A knowing glance, a silent understanding,
In these moments, love's true essence begins.

A whispered "I love you" in the dead of night,
When the world is hushed and dreams take flight.
A tender kiss upon a weary brow,
Soothing the worries, easing the here and now.

In the rush of life, these moments may seem small,
But their significance shines above it all.
For in these delicate threads, love is found,
Binding hearts together, forever bound.

So let us not forget the beauty they hold,
These overlooked moments, more precious than gold.
For love's true magic lies within these whispers,
The small, forgotten moments, forever cherished.

Symphony of Love

Let the symphony of love begin,
A composition of emotions deep within.
Like a grand orchestra, we shall play,
Each movement representing a different phase.

The first movement, a lively allegro,
A burst of joy and passion that starts to grow.
Crescendos of laughter and smiles so bright,
As we dance together, our hearts take flight.

Then comes the second, a gentle adagio,
A tender melody, a moment of sorrow.
Whispers of sadness, tears softly fall,
But our love remains strong, standing tall.

The third movement arrives, a scherzo so fun,
Laughter and playfulness, like rays of sun.
We chase each other in a joyful dance,
Creating memories, taking a chance.

And now the finale, a grandioso display,
A culmination of love in every way.
The harmonious blend of everyday life,
Where love endures, conquering all strife.

The symphony of love, a masterpiece divine,
With movements that intertwine.
From the highs of joy to the lows of sorrow,
Our love's symphony will continue to borrow.

So let us embrace this symphonic affair,
With love as our melody, we'll always share.
For in this symphony, our hearts are entwined,
A love that's eternal, forever defined.

Love Library

In this vast library of love,
A myriad of books, like stars above.
Romance whispers from the shelves,
As passion weaves its magic spells.

First, a book of adventure takes its place,
We embark on a journey, hand in hand, with grace.
Together we conquer mountains high,
And sail across oceans beneath the sky.

Next, a book of comedy, full of laughter and joy,
Our love a source of mirth that none can destroy.
With witty banter and playful jest,
We find solace in each other's best.

But amidst the laughter, a book of drama unfolds,
The conflicts and trials that our love beholds.
Through tears and heartache, we find our way,
Stronger together, come what may.

And then, a book of romance, pure and true,
With tender moments and whispered "I love you."
Passionate kisses and longing embraces,
Our love written in the most delicate of graces.

But let us not forget the other genres, my love,
For our library of love is vast and thereof.
Mystery, fantasy, and even suspense,
Each chapter filled with intense suspense.

As we turn the pages of our love's library,
We discover new genres, filled with endless possibility.
Our love story, a masterpiece in its own right,
A collection of books that shines so bright.

So let us cherish this metaphorical library,
Where our love's narratives are bound for eternity.
In every chapter, we find something new,
A love that is diverse, rich, and true.

Elemental Love

In the realm of love, Earth stands strong,
A foundation of stability, where hearts belong.
Solid and grounding, it brings us together,
Nurturing the roots of love, forever and ever.

But love cannot thrive on stability alone,
Air, the element of communication, must be known.
Whispering words of affection, like a gentle breeze,
It carries our feelings, putting our hearts at ease.

Fire ignites the passion that burns within,
An element that kindles desire, a flame that can't dim.
With fiery kisses and embraces so warm,
Love blazes brightly, defying any storm.

Yet, love is not just a flame that burns bright,
Water, the element of emotion, adds depth to the sight.
Like a gentle river, it flows through our veins,
Expressing love's essence, washing away all pains.

Earth provides stability, Air fosters connection,
Fire fuels passion, Water stirs deep affection.
In this dance of elements, love finds its way,

Creating a symphony of emotions, day by day.

Together, Earth, Air, Fire, and Water,
They shape the journey of love, each a daughter.
Bound in a cosmic dance, they intertwine,
Creating a love story that is truly divine.

So let us embrace the elements of love's lore,
And let our hearts be forevermore.
For in this symphony of Earth, Air, Fire, and Water,
We find a love that is pure, eternal, and ever-after.

Celestial Love

In the vast expanse of the cosmic night,
Our love shines like constellations bright.
A tapestry of stars, we intertwine,
Creating beauty that is truly divine.

Like meteor showers, we collide and ignite,
Leaving trails of passion in our celestial flight.
Each moment spent together, a shooting star,
A rare and precious sight, no matter how far.

Our love aligns like planets in perfect harmony,
A cosmic dance, a symphony of unity.
We orbit each other, in an eternal embrace,
Bound by love's gravity, in a celestial chase.

The grandeur of our love knows no bounds,
It transcends the vastness of the universe, it astounds.
Rare and precious, like a celestial gem,
Our love shines brightly, a priceless diadem.

So let us bask in the awe-inspiring light,
Of a love that's grand, a love that's infinite.
For in the cosmic tapestry, our love will endure,
Forever shining bright, forever pure.

Love in a Time Capsule

In a time capsule, our love does reside,
Moments and memories, forever by our side.
Tokens of affection, cherished and true,
Representing the journey we've traveled through.

A photograph, frozen in time's embrace,
Capturing the radiance of your smiling face.
A handwritten note, penned with love's ink,
Each word a testament to the love we think.

A delicate flower, pressed with care,
Symbolizing the beauty we both share.
A worn-out ticket, from our first date,
A reminder of the sparks that ignited fate.

A mixtape of songs, that spoke our hearts,
Melodies that forever bind our parts.
A seashell, collected on a sandy shore,
Whispering the echoes of love forevermore.

A lock of hair, a strand of devotion,
Bound together, in eternal emotion.
A love letter, sealed with a passionate kiss,
Unveiling the depths of our eternal bliss.

These treasures within our time capsule's core,
Tell the tale of a love worth fighting for.
Through the ups and downs, we've remained strong,
In this time capsule, our love forever belongs.

May our story inspire others to cherish,
The love they have, and never let it perish.
For in this time capsule, our love is sealed,
A testament to a love that's truly revealed.

As the years go by, and the memories grow,
Our time capsule will forever show,
The essence of our love, pure and true,
Encapsulated for eternity, me and you.

Physics of Love

In the realm of our love, gravity abounds,
A force that pulls us close, never to be found,
Like celestial bodies locked in an eternal dance,
Our souls entwined, in a cosmic romance.

Just as gravity binds the stars in the sky,
Our love binds us, you and I,
With a magnetic force that's impossible to resist,
We're drawn together, forever intertwined, never to desist.

Energy flows through our veins, like an electric current,
Powering our love, with a fervent ardor that's permanent,
With every beat of our hearts, a symphony of passion,
Creating a pulse of love, in a rhythmic fashion.

Like the laws of motion, we move in perfect sync,
Each step we take, a dance, a graceful link,
Our love propels us forward, in a constant motion,
An unstoppable force, with a boundless devotion.

And just as light travels through the vast expanse,

Our love shines bright, with a radiant brilliance,
Illuminating our souls, with a celestial glow,
A love that transcends, for eternity to bestow.

So let our love be a testament, to the laws of the universe,
A fusion of physics and emotions, an eternal verse,
For in the dynamics of our relationship, we find,
A love that defies gravity, and forever intertwines.

About the Author

Sayan Panda

Sayan Panda, a talented author hailing from the vibrant city of Kolkata, has captivated readers with his imaginative storytelling. With a background in English literature and a passion for the written word, Panda has established himself as a noteworthy voice in the literary world. Having already published six books across various genres, he now ventures into unexplored territory, delving into the realms of the paranormal and the macabre. This foray into the mysterious and eerie showcases Panda's versatile storytelling abilities and his willingness to push the boundaries of his craft. Alongside his writing endeavors, Panda also dedicates himself to educating young minds as a dedicated school teacher.

www.ingramcontent.com/pod-product-compliance
Lightning Source LLC
LaVergne TN
LVHW041641070526
838199LV00053B/3493